SHE GOT ME

Deja

JUST BAE

"You are somebody's reason to smile."

— THE NEXT

CONTENTS

Chapter One

NO, SHE DIDN'T

"I can't do this, Malik. I just can't." Deja's wringing her hands together speaking quietly, playing with the basic gold band that encircles her left ring finger, turning and turning it around her thin finger-it still doesn't feel right, feel comfortable. "I thought I could do this... I tried Malik, I really did... but..."

Malik bites at his lower lip, worrying at it, not entirely sure what to say or what to do-he knows things aren't perfect-far from it, but they have to try. Have to keep trying-if only for Jasmine's sake. "Deja, I know it's hard. And... and I know that this isn't ideal, but..." and Malik's eyes sweep towards their bedroom and back to Deja's sad brown eyes.

She wilts, her features pained, tears filling her eyes. "I

know, Malik. Trust me, I know. But..." and Deja takes a deep breath before continuing. "I don't love you, Malik." The ring slides off over her knuckle between her right thumb and index finger. "And I'm not sure I can. Or if I ever will." She places the gold band on the edge of the coffee table.

It's not exactly a surprise to Malik, not really, but there's Jasmine-four-month old Jasmine laying in her bassinet sleeping peacefully in their bedroom, blissfully unaware in her infancy that just steps away in the living room her mother is facing one of the hardest decisions she'll ever make in her life.

"But... I love you Deja. Jasmine loves you, Deja." Malik says softly as he reaches for her hand. She pulls back, instead wrapping her fingers back together again and she won't meet his pleading eyes. "Deja... please..."

There are a thousand thoughts swimming around in Deja's head and she knows she's made her decision though and she knows that if she stays, it won't get better-she won't get better. Long nights, long days, and it's not going to get better once Malik's in and out and away on work for days at a time. She had thought it might change once Jasmine came-the depression, the anxiety, replaced with unconditional love and the overwhelming instinct to mother and care and protect-but it didn't. Instead, Deja found herself slipping further and further from those feelings-yes, she loves Jasmine, loves her more than she ever thought she could love anything-but underneath that love is fear, stress, panic, and most of all the deep sinking feeling of depression that just won't quit. Sleepless nights and days filled with Jasmine's crying and constant need for attention that's inherent to babies, chipping away at the last threads keeping Deja together. "I... I just can't, Malik..." And Deja folds in on herself, quiet sobs shaking at her shoulders as she sits hunched over.

"I..." Malik reaches tentatively for Deja's shoulder, hand hovering, unsure what's really happening here-does he comfort her? Tell her it's going to be ok? That they can make this work, figure it out? He's completely lost and the only thing he can do is focus on his male nature to fix, solve, and repair. "We..."

Deja cuts him off, voice quivering. "Malik, don't... You can't. We can't." She looks up, tears still spilling down her cheeks. "I can't." She gets up, turning, and heads off to the bedroom and closes the door behind her while Malik's left sitting on the couch trying to stop his world from spinning.

A short while later, Deja emerges, suitcase dragging

behind her and she stops in the doorway to the living room. "Make sure Jasmine has a bottle at 3 and use the crème when you change her." Her soft brown eyes meet Malik's one last time and she heads for the door. "I'll call you in a few days. We'll... Just let Jasmine know I love her and take good care of her."

Malik watches from the couch as Deja walks out the front door and he puts his head in his hands and cries quietly.

Chapter Two

WHAT'S UP? I'M INTO YOU

"Go talk to her for God's sake, Malik." DeShawn cuffs his brother upside the head, making him spill a bit of his beer over the top of the red Solo cup. "You've been watching her for like an hour."

DeShawn's right. As soon as she had shown up at the party-'friend-of-a-friend', Logan told him Malik hadn't been able to keep himself from seeking her out. His eyes following her movements as she drifted from group to group, always a couple steps behind her friends. She wasn't exactly a wall-flower, but Malik noticed that she stood at the perimeter of whoever was talking and laughed every now and then when the group did, but didn't seem to interject too much to keep the conversation going. It didn't seem to bother those around her-they just kept circulating the patio with this girl trailing along behind, every once in a while, checking to see if she needed another beer. "She, uh... she doesn't really look like she wants talk..." Malik waves his hand in her general direction showing DeShawn how she's just standing looking around the room aimlessly.

"Bull Malik. You don't know that. Maybe she's just shy.... *Sort of like someone else I know...*" DeShawn punctuates his last statement with another cuff to the head.

"I don't know..." But Malik finds himself being pushed from behind, DeShawn's hand shoving between his shoulder blades as he tries not to stumble over his own feet. "Ok... ok..."

"Uh... good party, huh?" Malik fumbles for words when he finds himself standing in front of this girl-average height, short brown hair, brown eyes, slight tan to her skin, not fake, just gathered from countless hours out in the hot Texas sun.

She looks up at him, tilting her head to meet his big brown uncertain eyes looking down at her from almost a foot above. "For sure." She doesn't offer any more and Malik sort of just shifts from foot to foot.

"It's my birthday."

"Yeah, gathered that from the banner..." She turns her brown eyes up and to the left.

Malik winces inwardly-stupid, he berates himself, of course she'd know that, why else would she be there, hanging on his patio literally three feet from the big 'Happy Birthday Malik' sign that DeShawn had so graciously hung over the sliding door. "Um..."

"Sorry..." She says. "Sarcasm's my default setting..." She holds her beer tight to her chest. "I'm... not great at social stuff..." She shrugs as she talks.

"Yeah, me neither..." Malik counters. "But, ah, thanks for coming out tonight." Really? Like she's a guest on a TV show? "I mean..."

"I get it." A hint of a smile breaks across her lips. "Nice place." She gestures with her cup at the stone patio, the backyard-sparse, but well taken care of. "Nice view of the city."

Malik looks out over the back fence and nods. The lit up glowing outline of the city-not too close, but not too far-was one of the reasons he picked this condo. That and the nice secluded fenced in back yard. A tiny oasis for peace in his increasingly busy life. "

Yeah... it's nice back here. Like to come out at night and just relax and stuff."

"Looks like it's good for that."

"Yeah..." He doesn't say much more and they stand together, side by side, sipping their beers, just watching the lights in the city sparkle as dusk turns to night.

After a relatively quiet while, aside from a few interruptions of 'Happy Birthday' and 'Here's to you, Malik, Malik turns to the girl. "I didn't get your name."

"Oh..." She looks down towards her shoes, toeing at the little pebbles filling the cracks between the patio stones. "It's Deja."

"I'm Malik."

"Yeah... it's your birthday." She points to the sign again. "We covered that."

Lord... is he socially inept or what? Malik kicks himself mentally and groans to himself. No wonder he's single. "Um... yeah. Sorry." His cheeks flush just slightly, embarrassment setting in.

She reaches over and gives him a little punch in the arm. "It's ok." She smiles. "We're pretty bad at this, aren't we?"

Malik just nods. "Um... you want to go in? Grab another beer? I could show you around the place? Show you the, uh, inside."

Deja accepts and steps over the threshold separating the patio from the living room as Malik holds the sliding screen door out of her way. "Nice..." She lets her eyes roam over the furniture, the pictures on the wall, and the entertainment center. "Looks comfortable in here."

It does. Malik spent a long time-too long according to DeShawn (who was dragged along when he came up for a visit) - picking out just the right sofa with the right amount of cushioning, a dark, but not too dark, entertainment center, and somewhat serene looking wall art-scenes of the city at night, pictures of his home town in the winter, and just sweeping landscapes of indiscriminate places. "I like to just veg in here when I get home."

Deja nods approvingly and makes her way over to the small kitchen and rests her elbows on the little breakfast bar that separates the two rooms. She looks over at the kitchen table, nestled in the corner and covered in various bills, t-shirts, and empty beer bottles. "Don't eat in here much, huh?"

"Nah. I live alone. Not much sense in setting the table for

one. You know?" Malik shrugs. "I usually just heat something up and eat on the couch."

"Me too."

Malik smiles at her as he reaches into the fridge to pull out
another couple beers. He takes her cup, places it next to
his on the countertop and pops open the bottles, filling
both the cups so the foam is just about to spill over the lip.
"C'mon, I'll show you the rest of the place. It's not too big,
but there's a little more."

Deja follows as Malik takes her down the carpeted hallway, pointing out the bathroom on the right (privately
thanking himself that he remembered to clean up the pile
of boxers and for once, remembering to put the seat
down). "Bathroom." He indicates with a wave of the hand.
"Um... in case you need it or something."

"I'm good." She smiles.

"That's the spare room." He swings the door open.
"DeShawn usually comes up when he can, so he stays in
here." Explaining the handful of baseball caps and
random t-shirts littering the floor. "He's up here for a few
days cause..."

"Cause it's your birthday, right?" Deja chuckles.

Malik laughs too. "Yeah..."

They may be exceptionally awkward-but Malik's having a good time, he likes it when she smiles. And he finds he really likes her laugh. He hopes she's at least having a not terrible time with him. "So, um... last room's my bedroom. Ah..." He steps back out in the hallway, unsure if it's cool or whatever to show her. He doesn't want her to get the wrong impression.

"Cool." She seems amenable to the idea as she comes out into the hallway to stand next to Malik whose hand is hovering over the doorknob. "You gonna open it? Or let me just use my x-ray vision?"

That elicits a startled laugh from Malik, the high pitched dorky giggle escaping. He looks over at Deja who's laughing now too. She mimics a pair of binoculars and stares straight at the bedroom door. "Let's see-unmade bed... check. Full hamper. Check... Yep. Definitely a guy's room."

"C'mon, it's not that bad." Malik protests and opens the door. Ok. Fine. The bed isn't made, but at least the covers aren't on the floor, and sure, the hampers full, but in his defense, it's been a busy week, what with DeShawn there and preparing for the party. And really, he wasn't actually expecting to show anyone, let alone a girl, his room. Deja surveys the bedroom, raising her eyebrow at him as she looks at the bed, then the hamper. "I told you I had x-ray vision."

Malik rolls his eyes. She punches him again lightly in the arm and he fakes the pain, wincing and grabbing at his bicep. "Aw, did I hurt you?" Deja plays it up too, leaning in and wrapping her fingers over Malik's on his arm. "I have super strength too..." She grins up at him and gives a little squeeze as her hand lingers over his. Malik tips his head down, eyes bright with laughter and his breath catches just a little bit when their gazes meet, her light brown eyes, crinkled just a tiny bit around the edges because of her wide smile. He bites down on his lower lip, suddenly nervous, darts just the tip of his tongue out and over the bow of his upper lip and just... just looks down at her. Something in her face changes, the smile, seconds ago full of mischief and mirth, now softening, turning just to this side of shy, and she parts her lips just slightly.

"Uh..." Malik lets out a little noise, not really even a word, just more of a sound, and they both stand looking at each other, timid, awkward, and Malik seizes the moment - it's his birthday after all-and closes the distance between them and really really softly just rests his lips against hers. He feels her fingers tighten on his hand, his hand that's still wrapped around his bicep, and he brings his other arm up and places his palm flat against the curve of her lower back as he presses his kiss a little more firmly on her lips. He feels the give of her mouth, feels her lean imperceptibly up and in, meeting the push with a push of her own, and he pulls her in closer with the hand on her back.

Deja rises up on her toes, meeting Malik's kiss and slides her hand up to rest against his muscular shoulder. She uses her other hand to nudge his fingers off of his own bicep and guides it down to rest on swell of her hip. The kiss is slow and soft, their mouths just sort of moving together and she sneaks her eyes open to peek at Malik and thinks to herself 'he's cute' as he's leaned in, big brown eyes behind closed lids, dark brown hair flopping down over his forehead, tickling at her eyebrows.

Malik feels her hands on his arms and his nerves just melt away. He uses his tongue to gently lap at her lips, teasing and poking the tip just fractionally into her mouth and he feels her mouth open more, feels her tongue tentatively reaching out to meet his. He runs the tip up and over her tongue, feeling her teeth, feeling her warm breath puffing out around their joined mouths. Malik takes a slow step forward, guiding Deja backwards bit by bit, hoping he's not pushing it, until he feels her knees hit the mattress behind them. "You good?" He mutters against her lips and waits to feel the nod of her head before gently letting her down on the edge. Deja scoots her body up the bed, hands sliding down to wind into the soft fabric of Malik's tee and she pulls him along as she lies down.

His breath is quickening, he's really turned on, their lips aren't parting and she's got handfuls of his t-shirt in her fists and she's pulling him over her body as she's getting herself comfortable on the bed. Malik crawls up the mattress, knees on either side of her body, arms holding himself up as they come to rest fully on the bed. Malik feels her hands release the soft cotton of his shirt and shivers inadvertently when the delicate tickle of her nails drags slowly up and under the hem of his tee. Her hands are warm and her nails short and she lightly runs the pads of her fingers around his sides and up his back. Malik slides his lips away from hers, softly mouths along her cheek, down her jawbone, and up to the tender spot beneath her ear. He kitten licks at the lobe, sucks gently at the skin below-not hard enough to leave a mark-and makes his way down her lightly tanned neck to the thick strap of her tank top.

Deja roams her fingers all over Malik's broad back, feels his warm skin under her hands, and she pulls him closer, urging him down. She's wearing flip flops and kicks them off, soft thunks as they fall over the edge onto the carpet below. She runs her toes up the back of Malik's calves, down the sides, just aimlessly caressing at his legs with her feet. Deja pushes her fingertips into the muscles that play across Malik's back, likes the feel under her hands of strength; strong, and secure. She feels Malik's mouth, his tongue tasting every inch of her neck, her collarbone, slipping under the strap of her tank and she lets out a small sigh when she feels his teeth nipping along. Deja feels Malik's hand up and up, and feels when he slides it over to her side, and he leaves it, resting just below the swell of her breasts, his thumb rubbing gently along her ribs through the tank.

Malik feels the slight ribbed texture of Deja's tank under this thumb, feels the cotton ridges as he drags over and over, occasionally feeling the stiff sculpture of her underwire. His eyes drift down and she's got her eyes closed, head tipped back and he sneaks a quick look down at himself and kind of cringes when he realizes that the thin basketball shorts he chose to wear earlier are doing absolutely nothing to hide his erection. He hopes she doesn't notice. Or he does. He doesn't know. He's over thinking the whole thing when he feels one of Deja's hands remove itself from under his shirt and grab him lightly by the wrist as she urges his hand up and on to her breast. Malik sinks down, coming to rest with his side on the bed, arm crooked under his head, leaning in partially covering

Deja's body with his own. He knows at this point his erection is probably pretty noticeable, pressing up against her thigh, but he tries not to think about it, but thinks instead about how round and soft and just good her breast feels.

He traces the outline of her bra with his index finger, runs it over the barely noticeable ridge under the tank while slowly mouthing again at her neck, jawbone, and lips. It's slow and leisurely and he lets her set the kind of pace she wants, afraid that if he goes too fast he'll go too far, come off too eager, and he doesn't want to do anything that's going to end this any sooner than it has to.

Deja shifts, turns in towards Malik and throws her leg over his, hooking her calf behind his knee and pulls him closer; she definitely feels him hard pressing against her thigh and she thinks it's hot, so she gives a little push, rubbing the meat of her thigh up against his groin. Malik groans in to her mouth, a soft, wanting kind of noise. She bites at his lips as she plays with the hem of his shirt, twisting it and threading it between her fingers, dipping her fingertips down to brush against the waistband of his shorts and he pushes back against her thigh as she does so. She feels his hand, palm wide cupping her breast, holding it, using his fingers to massage lightly across the top and she covers that hand with her own and guides it up and under her tank. "Malik..." Deja breathes his name into his mouth and rubs against his groin again, feeling the hardness and feeling the shudder of arousal coursing through her.

Her breasts are warm and just... perfect, Malik thinks. He dips his thumb under the line of her bra, pulls it down so he can rub at her nipple, feeling it harden under the pads of his fingers. He rolls it between his thumb and forefinger, feeling her squirm and breathe harder and harder into his mouth. Her hands are down, definitely under his waistband now, fingers digging into his hips and into the small dip around his hip bone. He lets out a small giggle when her fingers brush against the join of his leg, the touch so light it actually tickles. He can feel her smiling against his mouth. "You good?" He mumbles into her lips while his fingers roam over her breasts, pinching at her nipples every now and then. He gets his answer when her hand wraps around his erection and she slowly moves her fist loosely up and down over the cotton of his boxers. He smiles back against her mouth.

Things move quicker after that. Malik rocks his hips into Deja's touch and he bites and sucks at her neck, making her moan and whine, moaning himself when she drags her thumb up over his cotton covered hardness and rubs at the growing wet spot on his boxers. Malik pulls back a bit, sits up a little and pulls Deja up with strong arms. He grabs the hem of her tank and slides the shirt up over her head, mussing up her short hair in the process so it's sticking up at the top in little spiky tufts. She moves her hands and self-consciously kind of pats it back in to place, but he stops her. "It's cute like that..." And she blushes. Malik reaches around to her back, and fumbles a little with the hooks on her bra, mostly out of nervousness and anticipation, but gets the first one popped, then the second, and he helps her out of it as she shimmies her shoulders a little to let it slide down and off her arms. Malik pulls his own shirt over his head and immediately feels her fingers sliding over his smooth chest and down over his barely there abs. He's a little too turned on to feel any kind of awkward about his not sculpted body, and Deja doesn't seem to mind anyway so he moves his hands down to the button of her shorts.

Deja shivers a little as soon as her tank and bra are off, not so much cold as just exposed and turned on and anticipating what's to come. Maybe it's the beer, maybe it's just the newness and the excitement but she feels a little heady and she feels goosebumps running down her arms when Malik just looks at her and she feels his fingers land on her shorts button. Malik gives her an unspoken questioning look, asking her if what he's doing is ok, just like he's done every time they've taken this up a notch. And she appreciates it. A lot. She nods at him, eyes sparkling and smile playing at the corners of her mouth, and she holds her breath when he pops the button and slides the zipper down tooth by tooth.

Malik gently pushes Deja back down on the bed and grabs the waistband of her shorts between his fingers and slides them down over her hips, revealing simple cotton panties with a small geometric pattern covering the material. He brings the shorts down over her knees, and down off over her feet and they land with a muffled thump off the end of the bed. He tries to take his time working his way back up her legs, just dragging his fingers over her tanned skin, but he's getting a little antsy, he's really hard, and he's really turned on and he really just wants to get close to her, and hold her, and feel her holding him back. As he gets closer to her, he feels her hands tugging at his shorts, and he feels a little stupid that he didn't just take them off when he was at the end of the bed. But he shucks them now, sliding them off and tossing them wherever, and gets himself so he's got Deja's legs between his knees and he's back down holding himself over her, hair flopping down over his forehead.

"You, um..." Malik makes a face he really hopes relays 'you want to have sex with me?' without him actually having to go so far as to say it. Deja nods beneath him and pulls him close, hand on the small of his back pressing him into her so they rock and grind together, cotton panties against cotton boxers.

Deja feels Malik hard and heavy against her and she feels everything so heightened; every touch of Malik's big hands, every breath hot against her neck. She's wet, can feel it warm between her legs and can't help letting out little moans when she feels them pushing together, little throbs of pleasure centered right where Malik's hardness slides up the front of her panties. She clears her throat a little, "you got..."

Malik knows what she's saying and he nods, pushing back with his arms to turn and rummage through the drawer of his nightstand. As he comes back, Deja reaches down and takes off her panties and Malik just takes a moment to run his fingers down her stomach and down to touch lightly at her inner thighs. He feels her hands reaching for his boxers and he helps her pull them off, crumpling them and kicking them off the bed. Malik looks down at Deja again, and she's looking back, eyes soft and hopeful, half-lidded with arousal and he tears the top off the package and slides the condom out between his fingers. He pinches the tip, lines it up against his erection and unrolls the slippery latex down his length with his thumb and forefinger. "You, ah... ready?" She nods.

Malik positions himself between Deja's legs, nudges her knees a little further apart with his knees, and bends down, one hand on the base of his erection, the other resting on the bed, fingers splayed, off to Deja's side. She shifts a little, helping him line up and he pushes, gently, slowly, feeling the warmth as he slides in. Malik feels Deja's hands on his sides, pulling him down and closer, and he slides in a bit more, a bit more, until he's fully in and both his hands are framing her head. He pivots his hips, and Deja rocks beneath him, hands firm across his back and he leans down to kiss her.

Deja feels Malik filling her up, feels him pushing in deeper and deeper, sliding and pulls him close. He smells like sweat and deodorant and it's just nice. Comforting. Something about his broad shoulders and his hands framing her head gives her a quiet sense of security. And she knows he's gentle and he's going to make sure she's ok. She spreads her fingers out over his back, feeling at the swell of his ass as he pushes in and pulls out and she soon lifts her legs up to hook around his thighs and uses them to pull him in deeper and harder. She watches his face, his lips parted, eyes closing then opening, watching her, blinking. Always giving that little questioning look before going harder or faster. Always making sure she's ok.

Malik grunts and pushes in and out, sweat beading on his

forehead and along his temple and he sees Deja beneath him with her eyes looking back at him glazed with arousal. Her legs wrap around his thighs and he's pulled closer and closer, and he leans down and he covers her with wet sloppy kisses. His tongue pushes into her mouth, uncoordinated because of his thrusting and he feels her nails digging into his back as she urges him on, harder and faster. He closes his eyes and concentrates on the warm enveloping feel of Deja around his hardness, on the sharp sting of nails in his back, and the tight hold she has around the backs of his thighs. Malik hears her quietly chanting his name over and over, Malik... Malik... Malik... and he feels her starting to tighten occasionally around him. Each little burst of snugness around him sends a pulse through him and he can feel himself getting closer and closer.

Deja feels Malik strong and solid above her and feels him sliding in and out, hard and thick and fast. She tilts her hips up a little, repositions so Malik's inward thrusts are rubbing in just the right places and she feels the tingling and sensitive jolts and she's breathing out his name over and over as she feels the tingles spreading outwards. She pulls him in to her hard hard hard and fast fast fast and then lets out an indiscriminate whine-sigh-moan and holds him hard against her with her legs as she pulses around him. And it's sensitive, so sensitive, as he slowly starts to thrust again, and she talks to him, urging him on, whispering his name.

Malik feels Deja tighten down around him and feels her heels digging into his thighs when he's held tight against her and he waits for her to come down before slowly starting up again. He hears her whispering, c'mon babe, so good, come for me... and it doesn't take much longer before his timing is off, and his hips are moving unevenly and he holds himself against her as he feels himself coming and he's so lost in the feeling that he doesn't actually realize it feels a little different than every other time he's come. He catches his breath and reaches down to hold the base of the condom as he pulls out and he blanches.

It's wet. Like, a lot wetter than it should be. And shit. The condom broke and Malik's pulling out and his come is just kind of all over the outside of the condom and a little bit drips down onto the bed beneath and he grimaces and stutters. "Shit...um... shit..." His eyes are panicked.

"Um... shit what, Malik?" Deja's immediately propped up on her elbows, taking in the look in Malik's eyes and feeling her chest tightening as he's still got his hand on the base of his now soft penis and one hand resting on her knee. And she realizes that yeah, she's really really wet and not in a good way. "Oh god... did it...?"

"Yeah..."

"Fuck..." Deja's eyes fill with tears. "Fuck!" She slumps back down onto the bed and then jumps up, grabbing at her tank on the floor and hopes to God no one's in the hallway when she runs into the bathroom.

Malik hears the door slam behind her and he's left, kneeling on the bed, broken condom just sort of there and he doesn't know what the fuck to do.

Chapter Three

WHAT'S THE DEAL?

They see each other sometimes after that, dates, dinner, just hanging out, but it's always kind of muted, awkward, that big question of, 'are you?' 'am I?' hanging in the air between them. Deja takes a pregnancy test about two weeks after Malik's birthday, one of the 'early detection' kind found at the drugstore, and it's over lunch one afternoon that she tells Malik.

"I'm not pregnant."

The worry lines in Malik's forehead-the ones that had been a constant since *that* night-seem to fade as Deja speaks. He lets out his breath with a sigh of relief. It's not that he doesn't want to be a father; he just doesn't want to be a father right now. And he's not even sure if he wants to be a parent with Deja. Sure, he likes her, but it's still new and it kind of got off to a shaky start and he's only just turned twenty three and she's only twenty so, it's really not the right time at all.

* * *

The next few weeks seem to go a little better. They're hanging out a bit more frequently as mid-August comes and Malik finds he likes Deja more and more each day-still not love, but if he had to put it in to words, it would be along the lines of 'really really really like'. They're just hanging out in his condo, take-out containers scattering the top of his coffee table, when she turns to look at Malik. "I'm late."

"You're... what?" Malik heard her. He's pretty sure he knows what she's getting at. But it can't be. The test was false. She told him it was false.

"I'm late." There aren't tears in her eyes, but the look she's got definitely isn't a happy one. It's not angry either though-it's really just kind of sad, and scared. "I made a doctor's appointment for later in the week."

"Uh... ok." What's the protocol here? Offer to go with her? Step back? Malik doesn't know-it's not like he's ever really been in this type of situation before so he settles for not saying anything else. If she wants him there, she'll tell him.

"I'll let you know what happens. You don't have to go with me or anything." Question answered. Malik nods and tells her to call him right after and whatever comes of it, they'll figure it out.

"I'm pregnant, Malik." Deja pauses. "Pregnant."

Malik sits there, surprised and in shock, but not really-when she had said she was late he had kind of steeled himself for the day she'd tell him this. He'd called DeShawn that afternoon-after she said 'I'm late' and proceeded to melt down bit by bit until he was literally just mumbling 'oh god oh god oh god' into the phone and DeShawn had made the three hour drive up from Austin to talk some sense back into his brother.

"Pregnant." Malik repeats it, sounding the word out like he's never said it before. "So..." He's not sure what to say-he's never great with words, but especially now, he's completely useless with his vocabulary.

"Yeah." Silence stretches between them while Malik

opens and closes his mouth a few times, almost speaking but never finding the right words.

A few more moments go by, both of them just looking at each other, kind of feeling the other one out, hoping the other will say something-anything. Malik is the first to finally get anything remotely like words out of his mouth. "Are you gonna... uh... keep it?"

Deja shrugs. "I... I don't know." She looks down at her feet, toes barely brushing the carpet as she sits, legs swinging off the end of Malik's bed. "I... don't know."

"I think I have to ask her to marry me, DeShawn." Malik states into the phone when he hears the 'hi' on the other end-no preamble to it. "It's the right thing to do."

There's a pause on the other end as DeShawn gathers his thoughts. "Well, you don't *have* to, Malik. Just because she's pregnant doesn't mean you have to marry her. You're twenty three."

"I know. I know. It's just... it feels like the right thing to do." Malik fidgets with the hem of his t-shirt as he talks, pulling and stretching at the fabric. "I don't want..." pause "my... kid... to grow up without its parents."

"It won't have to. You're still going to be there, Malik, right? It's not like you're abandoning her. Or them, I guess."

Malik thinks about it for a minute before speaking. "I know, it's just, like, this way I know they'll both be taken care of."

"You can still take care of them and not be married, you know." DeShawn's got his 'big brother' voice going now-reasonable and level headed. "And you're working moving up the corporate ladder. You're not going to be around a lot, especially when you get sent away on those long business trips. Does it really help it if you're married to her?"

Malik sighs. He's thought about that, he knows that once September really gets into full swing, then October with the new accounts he's going to be in and out-out more than in-and he just wants Deja and the baby to be secure and taken care of, and to him, the best way to do that is to marry her. He'll grow to love her, he knows he will-and for sure he'll love the baby, so there's that. "Yeah. It does. I can't really describe it, DeShawn. But I know that I'll feel better if I at least ask her. If the baby has my name then I know that it'll always be taken care of no matter what." Malik realizes that sounds pretty selfish-as if Deja couldn't raise their child, couldn't look after her without the presence of a husband-but, like he couldn't explain it to his brother, he can't really put into words to himself either what it is about being a 'family unit' that just makes him feel more comforted and secure in the whole situation.

"You do what you gotta do, Malik. You know I'm always here and I'm gonna back you up whatever you decide."

Knowing that helps-not that Malik didn't know that DeShawn would be there for him regardless-he just really needed to hear it from him. "Thanks, DeShawn. I mean it." They say their goodbyes and Malik heads out to Deja's place.

"So, um... I was thinking..." Malik's sitting on the floor at the base of Deja's recliner as she sits opposite him on the couch. He's picking at a few loose fibers in the rug idly as he gets his thoughts straight. "I was thinking maybe we should get married." The words rush out. "I mean... because of the baby and stuff." He adds, uselessly. She looks down at him, puzzled. "Like, I make a good amount of money, and I have insurance, and well... you could be on that insurance, and the baby too. And it would... um... I'd feel better if I knew you two were taken care of."

Deja sort of hums.

"I mean... I don't mean you wouldn't take care of you. Or the baby, but..." Malik trails off. He's really just digging a hole for himself. He knew this wouldn't ever come out the way he wanted it to; he just can't put his feelings into words the right way without sounding weird.

She hums again.

"I. You. Well. Baby. Uh."

"Malik. Stop talking." Deja shushes him. "Let me think."

Malik keeps picking at the rug while Deja sits back, leaning into the cushions, hands folded over her stomach. Should she? Does she want to? Deja's mind is racing. The condom breaking was a horrific shock. The false negative on the pregnancy test had been a big relief-that was until she was late. Then hearing the doctor's voice contradicting that test and telling her, yes, she was indeed pregnant, had been another shock. She'd gone up and down the emotional spectrum for days and days and the feeling she kept coming back to was scared. What Malik was offering was comforting-financial security, health insurance, the knowledge that he was trying to do what he thought was the right thing-Deja knows that no matter what, Malik will always try to do the right thing.

He had asked her permission every step of the way the night they met-even if it was just through a questioning look. He hadn't fist-pumped the air when they first found out they thought she wasn't pregnant-a lot of guys would have probably jumped for joy, Malik just quietly gave a sigh of relief. When she had told him she was late, and later that she was pregnant, he hadn't outright freaked out, or worse, bolted. He had accepted it. And when she wasn't sure if she was going to keep the baby, he didn't pressure her one way or the other; he had just told her, 'whatever you decide is the right choice'. His whole reaction to the situation was one of the reasons she'd ultimately decided to continue with the pregnancy. Deja knows deep down that no matter what happens, Malik will always be there and will always be there to take care of the baby.

Malik shifts uncomfortably on the floor. He wants to know what Deja's thinking, but her face isn't giving anything away. Maybe it was a stupid idea. Yes. It was stupid, he decides. It was a rash decision, selfish, and she doesn't need him to be tethered to her simply because of the baby. He silently berates himself when he hears Deja speak. "Yes."

"What?" He shakes his head, clearing his self-deriding thoughts.

"I said yes, Malik. I think it's the best thing." Deja slides down on to the floor and shuffles over to Malik's side. "We'll figure it all out eventually I guess."

Malik turns and pulls Deja into a big hug and just rests his forehead on her shoulder as he closes his eyes and just holds her tightly.

Chapter Four

BABE

"*D*eja..." Malik gently shakes Deja's shoulder. "Deja... you gonna get up today?" It's ten-thirty and Deja hasn't made much of an effort to get out of bed. "You got an appointment at noon."

Deja just rolls the other way, faces the wall and doesn't say anything.

"C'mon, Deja. I know you feel like shit, but you gotta go to the doctors. Maybe he can give you something for the, you know, barfing and stuff." He gives her another little shake.

"Go away, Malik."

Malik runs his hands down his face in frustration. It's one thing if Deja wants to stay in bed on any random day, but really, she's got an appointment, and he has to leave to get to the office and he can't just sit here and argue with her about getting up and getting to her appointment. Not again. "No." He says firmly and he drags the covers away from her clenched hands. "You have to get up."

"God, Malik. What the hell." Deja thumps her arms heavily on the bed, much heavier than really necessary Malik thinks, as she gets up and storms off to the bathroom. He hears the sound of retching a moment later, then a flush, and Deja storms back in to the bedroom. "I could have rescheduled. I feel like shit."

Malik sighs, he knows this has been tough on Deja-morning sickness that somehow stretches to the afternoon. The feeling of not getting enough sleep, never enough energy to do anything. He knows she's struggling, but he also knows that this is their baby-and if she's got a doctor's appointment, she needs to go. And he feels like shit that he can't be there for her as much as he knows he should. "I know, Deja. And I'm sorry you do. But, you already rescheduled once, and you really need to go." He pauses for a minute. "Do you want me to call and let them know I can't be there till later?"

Deja shakes her head no. She knows Malik's really doing his best, she knew going in to this that he would be scarce most of the time, and she appreciates that he's willing to do whatever he needs to for this to be ok. Sometimes she thinks that he'd actually give everything up if it meant being able to be there for her and the baby. But she can't let him do that. "No. It's ok. I'll go... I'll go..." But she doesn't seem to be making much of an effort to get ready to go.

Malik pushes his frustration down, tells himself he has no idea what she's going through, that he can't possibly know what any of this feels like, and that he's really just watching what's going on from the outside so instead of picking at her reluctance to get up, go out, just do *anything* he pushes it down and goes over to the dresser and pulls out a light sweater and a loose skirt for her. "You'll look pretty cute in this?" He hands it over to Deja tentatively and nudges her shoes over to her feet with his toes. He gets a grumbled 'thanks' in return as he's turning to go get ready himself.

Malik's finished up in the kitchen, just thrown the last few odds and ends into the dishwasher, tidying up really before he goes (the place seems to have taken on a general sense of disarray lately-dishes left in the sink, clutter just piling up on the coffee table, laundry just sort of laying half-folded in the living room). And it's not like he expects Deja to take over and cook and clean and do his laundry while he's gone, far from it, it's just that nothing seems to

fingers stroke
en from those
pathy. "I wish

ing now, why
 now, and it's
 matter how
ted or good
up, she's got a
 too, and she,
es. Deja feels
lers, rubbing
er shoulders
sts her fore-
nore.

e Deja's got
 off a quick
Deja sick." -
e wrapping
se. It hurts

his elbow

or they get into a big
nakes a bit of a produc-
t Malik asked for. He
but time after time he
rmones' and 'girl stuff'
it, just accepts it and
nd finishes folding the

om, to say goodbye and
dge of the bed, sweater
 her face as she cries and
e muffled sobs.

hes to kneel down at her
the sweater away from her

nands. "Everything..."

ation. "Deja, what is it?" He
er face and wipes her tears
 of his thumb. "I'll call. I'll be
hone in his pocket.

k." Deja's words come out in
ks between stuttered breaths.
inue.

"I know you feel rotten, Deja." Malik's
lightly at Deja's short hair. His features sof
of frustration to those of sadness and sym
there was something I could do for you."

Deja sighs. She doesn't know why she's cry
she's been crying for what seems like month
wearing on her. She's exhausted; it doesn't
much sleep she gets, she never feels res
anymore. Her stomach hurts from throwing
constant sour taste to her mouth because of it
plain and simple, just feels like shit-so she cri
Malik's hands in her hair, then on her should
patiently and comfortingly up and down h
and she leans in to his touch, leans in and re
head on Malik's shoulder and just cries some

Malik slides his phone out of his pocket whil
her head buried against his neck and he shoot
text to Logan-gonna be late. "Tell the guys. I
and slides the phone back into his pocket befor
his arms around Deja and just holds her clo
that he can't fix this.

* * *

"Happy Valentine's Day, Deja." Malik leans on

facing Deja as her eyes groggily open and brushes her short brown hair off of her forehead. He gets a mumbled grunt in return. "How you feeling?"

Deja sort of grimaces, tilts her head, giving a 'meh' sort of expression. She feels fat. She feels swollen. She has heart-burn, has to pee, and is tired-so tired. Weird dreams keep her tossing and turning all night and so does the baby's kicking. She isn't entirely sure she can handle two more months of this-but she is thankful-Malik's been so patient, so understanding-the best he can be when he's been in and out for month on end. "I'm ok." Deja mumbles.

"Want some breakfast? I can make you pancakes or waffles or something..."

Deja's tries to manage a small smile-even if Malik could actually pull off edible pancakes, Deja's not entirely sure she can manage something like that right now. "Cereal maybe?"

Malik leans in and gives her a small kiss on the tip of her nose before sliding out of bed and padding out into the small kitchen. He's glad he's got a day off. He's set to leave the next morning for a two week long business trip ending at his parents' home. He hates to leave Deja behind, but at this point, she can't travel. He wanted her to meet his parents, but he understands, they'll come down when the baby is born anyway so it's not really that big of a deal.

Malik putters around in the kitchen, waiting for the bread to toast before finally pouring the milk into Deja's bowl of cereal. He pours her a glass of juice and slices up an apple too before carefully arranging everything onto a little lap tray so he can give her breakfast in bed. As he's getting ready to bring everything back to Deja, he remembers the Valentine's Day card he has stuffed in his gear bag, so he pulls it out and sits down at the kitchen table. The card is simple, just hearts and arrows and stuff like that with some generic sentiment pre-printed on the inside in scripted lettering that makes it look a little fancier than it really is and Malik rests his pen below the words and thinks about what he wants to write.

"Happy Valentine's Day" seems way to simple and generic. But, "to my wife that I love and cherish each and every day" seems a little overboard and honestly, not at all like something Malik would say. He sits and thinks, tapping the pen against his lip, brows creased in thought-it shouldn't be this hard to find something-anything to say-but somehow it is. The last few months, Malik's struggled to find the right words for anything-when Deja's sick, he tells her it'll be ok, and she cries and says it won't be. If he tells her he understands, she yells back that he doesn't. If he doesn't say anything, she takes it as he doesn't care and she cries even more. There are days that he feels like he's entering a mine field when he has to talk to her, because he simply doesn't know the reaction he's going to get. But he loves her-and he knows that she's struggling, so he kind of just grits his teeth and tries to be supportive and just takes whatever she throws at him, hoping that eventually, once the baby comes, things will come around.

He settles on, 'Happy Valentine's Day, Deja. I know it's been tough on you and it's almost over. You're beautiful and I love you.' It's not poetic and it's not earth-shattering and romantic, but it's plain and simple and it's how Malik feels so he scribbles his name at the bottom and slides it into the envelope before placing it on the tray with her breakfast.

Deja slides herself up against the headboard, propped up by a couple pillows behind her back, and watches as Malik shuffles back into the bedroom, tray held firmly in his hands, his eyes trained on the juice that's just millimeters away from slopping over the side of the glass. He comes to the side of the bed and places the tray in her lap as he gives her a small kiss on the top of her sleep-mussed short hair. "Thanks, Malik." And Deja tips her head up to give Malik a soft kiss on his lips.

Deja reaches down and picks up the card and slides it out of the envelope. She opens it and reads it, looking up at Malik when she's done, and Malik's just looking back, with a hesitant look, holding his breath and Deja feels tears stinging in her eyes when she sees that look on Malik's face. She's been horrible-to him and to be around-crying, fighting with him, challenging everything, and it all comes down on her when she sees that look and reads his words and suddenly she feels terrible. Malik doesn't deserve that, he's been so understanding, he's just stood there and taken it when she screams and yells and accuses him of never being there-even though she knows he's there every chance he can get. He doesn't get angry, he doesn't yell back, he just stands there and takes whatever she's throwing at him, and tells her it will get better. She feels like shit in this moment-feels like she can't possibly deserve him and she cries.

Malik winces. He wants to say 'not again' and throw his hands up and walk out of the room. But he doesn't. He's trying so hard to say the right things, to do the right things, and he knows, he just knows that this is all going to pass, going to get better eventually-it has to, because he's talked with his mom and she's told him stories of how she was when she was pregnant with DeShawn and how she'd cry at nothing. And she'd tell him how patient and understanding his father was, and how no matter how bad it got, he'd always be there, comforting her and supporting her, and how things did get better. It's just that being young and pregnant was tough-you didn't know how to handle things, you didn't know everything was going to be ok because in those moments, it didn't seem like it would be. Malik's mom told him, 'you just can't understand what she's going through, but you need to be there for her-as much as you can-and you can't take it personally, Malik, she's just scared'. And he believes her.

"Deja..." Malik takes the breakfast tray and sets in on the nightstand and just pulls her close and strokes her hair and lets her cry.

Malik's hand is going to break. He just knows it. Deja's fingers are wrapped in a death grip around his and he can feel the bones grinding together each time she squeezes-harder and harder-strength belying her small frame. "C'mon Deja, just a little more..." He tries to be encouraging, and actively tries not to pass out at the same time. Blood and other things Malik can't even begin to figure out coming out of his wife is another. The nurse reassures him that everything is normal, Deja is doing fine, and surprisingly, so is he. He's told just to stand there, keep encouraging Deja, and their baby will be there, in time. Malik bites at his lip.

His hands tremble. Malik's nervous, sweating, excited, terrified, and proud all in the seconds it takes for him to clip through the tough umbilical cord connecting Jasmine to the no longer needed source of blood and nutrients that helped her grow into the amazing six-pound baby girl that's currently crying and making uncoordinated movements as she's quickly swaddled and handed over to her mother. Malik hardly knows what to say or do, so he does the only thing he can do, and stands there by Deja's side, just smiling and smiling, blinking back his own tears, looking down at his newborn daughter.

Chapter Five

WE HAVE A BABY

"Oh god, Malik, she's so tiny." DeShawn hovers around Malik, hands reaching out then pulling back, not entirely sure how to even go about holding the small blanketed bundle in Malik's arms. "Takes after Deja, huh..."

"Do you want to hold her or not?" Malik retorts with a scowl on his face but still takes a moment to gently place Jasmine into her uncle's arms, repositioning DeShawn's hands and arms just so before completely letting go of his daughter.

"Man, she's beautiful." DeShawn's expression is soft as he coos and babbles down at his little niece. "How's Deja doing?"

"Uh, she's doing ok. Tired mostly." Malik tries to hide the worry on his face, but DeShawn's known him his whole life and Malik knows he can't lie, so after a moment his face drops and he tells DeShawn how it really is. "DeShawn, I don't know. It's like... one minute she's fine. She's nursing Jasmine, changing her, you know, baby stuff... then like the next, she's locked herself in the bedroom with me and Jasmine on the outside and all I can do is hear her crying in there. And then Jasmine's crying. And I asked Deja what's wrong but she won't tell me. She just doesn't say anything."

DeShawn gives Malik a sympathizing look.

"DeShawn, I don't know what to do. I don't know what I'm doing. I... Jasmine needs her mother and it's like Deja is there, but not there." Malik looks exhausted and drained. "I just... I don't know how to fix all this."

"Maybe you can't."

"What?" Malik looks at DeShawn like he didn't quite hear him.

"Maybe you can't fix it. I dunno much about this stuff, but it doesn't really sound ok or anything. This isn't the first time you've said she's been like this." DeShawn shrugs.

"You called me all the time when she was pregnant telling me the same sh-stuff. Maybe she needs help."

"But, I am trying to help her, DeShawn. I've got Jasmine with me most of the time, I'm getting pretty good at getting her bottles and things when Deja won't breastfeed. And I can change her. I'm getting meals, doing laundry. DeShawn, I'm doing everything. I don't understand and I don't know what's wrong. And I *can't* fix it."

DeShawn kneels down and places Jasmine on the small blanket that's lying on the floor. He pulls Malik down on to the couch and sits down with him as he puts his hand on Malik's shoulder. "Malik. I don't mean you. I mean professional help."

"It's only been a week. She's probably just... tired. Or like, stressed or something. She's been through a lot." Malik's frustrated and discouraged, but as far as he's concerned, there's nothing really *wrong* with Deja. She's just over-tired and drained and she's always been emotional as long as he's known her. "There's nothing wrong with her-I mean that she'd need a shrink or something."

The look DeShawn gives Malik borders on exasperation. "Look, Malik. I'm not trying to be a dick. I'm not saying there's something *wrong* with Deja. I'm just saying maybe she could use someone to talk to about all this." Malik opens his mouth to speak but DeShawn cuts him off. "Someone that's not you. I know you want to help her, and you are. You're there for her even if she doesn't show it. You're doing all the things for her right now that she can't."

"Or won't..." Malik mumbles under his breath which gets him a sharp thump on his arm from DeShawn.

"Anyway, I can't pretend to know what it's like to be you or her right now. But from what you're telling me," DeShawn pauses, "and what you've been telling me *for months* is that something isn't right and it's not really getting any better. Take her to see someone, Malik. I know Mom will watch Jasmine while you do. She isn't just coming down here so she can cook you dinner and stuff you know. She's coming down to help you out-however you need it."

DeShawn's words are sobering. Malik's just been taking it and taking it for a long time now and he's always just figured that Deja was tired, pregnant, emotional-whatever. He doesn't know what it's like to go through everything she's gone through-he's just been along for the ride, doing anything and everything he can think of to take any burden off of Deja. Malik's told himself it's going to ok and why wouldn't it be? They've got a brand-new baby girl, he's got a career that will provide for all three of them, he's going to be here all summer and when he goes back to work, he's told Deja they'll get a nanny or something to help out while he's gone. But, and Malik stops and really thinks about it for a minute, maybe DeShawn is right. For everything he's been doing, he hasn't noticed any change in Deja. Malik slumps in his seat and brings his hands to his face. "Why aren't I good enough to fix it, DeShawn?"

DeShawn pulls Malik in, wraps his arms tight around him and holds him there. "Sometimes you just can't fix things, Malik." And DeShawn feels Malik crying softly against him.

Malik wakes up to feel a slight pressure squirming on his chest and he definitely feels a wet puddle pooling at the base of his throat. He opens his eyes and is greeted by Jasmine, two and half months old, laying on his chest, tiny fist in her mouth, drooling everywhere.

"Happy birthday, Daddy!" Deja leans in and whispers in to Malik's ear before placing a quick kiss on his temple. "Jasmine loves you."

Malik smiles a sleepy smile and rests his big hands across

Jasmine's small back and silently thanks whoever he can for his healthy, bright, squirmy little girl. The last two months (along with the previous nine) have been tough-very tough. But, after what Malik thinks is a surprisingly little amount of fighting with Deja, he'd been able to talk her in to going to see a psychologist, and he feels like things might be turning a corner. Sure, things still aren't perfect, and he's come to realize they probably won't ever be what he would consider 'normal' but Deja is doing better. It's much less frequent that she locks herself in the bedroom, and she's started sleeping a bit better, and she's even wanted to go out with Malik and Jasmine when he's taken her out and about for errands. Malik never thought that things like talking to someone and anti-depressants could really work as well as they seem to be. As much as he's had ups and downs in his life, he never felt it was something he couldn't handle, and he thinks back that it's probably why he had such a hard time realizing that he couldn't fix what was going on. Sometimes people just need a little extra help.

"What does Daddy want for breakfast for his birthday?" Deja speaks in a baby voice, head down close to Jasmine's, pretending it's their daughter asking the question.

Malik mulls it over. Neither of them are particularly good cooks, so when they're busy, Malik usually has a service delivering meals, but when he's freer, he generally stuffs the freezer with things like French toast sticks, pre-made breakfast sandwiches, and tons and tons of frozen pizzas (the kind with every kind of meat you can think of, with extra cheese, because, really, who doesn't want that?). "French toast sticks, coffee-a big cup of coffee-and... hmmm... you!" He takes Jasmine's little fist out of her mouth and pretends to nibble on her fist causing the little girl to coo and gurgle happily. It's really one of the best sounds in the world if you ask Malik.

Deja nods and picks Jasmine up from Malik's chest and makes her way into the kitchen to get breakfast heated up. They've got a little playpen set up that they can drag around from room to room, so Jasmine can always be with one of them and Deja places her on her back and gives the little mobile a tap so it starts turning and plinking out its little tune. From back in the bedroom, Malik can just hear the faint melody along with the various noises of the freezer opening, the little squeak the toaster makes when the lever is depressed, and soon the gurgle and hiss of the coffee maker doing its thing. He closes his eyes and just listens. It's not too long before he hears the pop of the toaster and he hears the clink of what he assumes is a plate and mug being taken from the cupboard and the smell of freshly brewed coffee wafts back into the bedroom. Malik

slides himself up in the bed, resting his back against the
headboard and is smoothing the sheet out over his thighs
when he hears it. A definite crash and shatter-the sound of
a mug hitting the floor and breaking and a second later,
the high-pitched squeal and wail coming from Jasmine.
He's out of bed and on his feet in a flash.

"Are you ok?" Malik rushes into the kitchen to find
Jasmine still in her playpen crying as loud as her little
lungs can manage, shards of broken coffee mug littering
the floor scattered in pools of cooling brown coffee, and
Deja, head down on the counter just crying softly. "You
ok, Deja? It's ok. It's just the coffee." Malik runs his hand
over her back. "Why don't you get Jasmine and I'll clean
this up, ok?" Deja just cries harder and runs to the
bedroom and Malik hears the door slamming behind her.
He swallows his frustration and goes to pick Jasmine up
from the playpen, holding her close and comforting her,
cooing in her ear softly that it's ok, it was just a loud noise,
and everything is going to be fine. He thinks a bit bitterly
to himself, it was nice while it lasted.

* * *

"Make sure Jasmine has a bottle at three and use the
diaper crème when you change her." Her soft brown eyes

meet Malik's one last time and she heads for the door. "I'll call you in a few days. We'll... Just let Jasmine know I love her and take good care of her."

Malik watches from the couch as Deja walks out the front door and he puts his head in his hands and cries quietly.

Chapter Six

DAMN!

"She left, DeShawn... she left..." Malik states into the phone, voice broken and rough. "She left me and Jasmine and I don't know what's going on. I don't know if she's coming back."

"God... Malik... you ok?" DeShawn hears the sadness and complete desperation in Malik's voice and it hurts him to know his younger brother is going through this. "Malik?" All he hears on the other end of the phone is shuddered breathing and small sniffs.

"No, it's not ok, *DeShawn*. My wife just left. She left me, and told me she didn't love me, and she left me with the baby." Malik's voice is getting louder, cracking and breaking as he speaks. "She put her fucking wedding ring on the table, told me she didn't love me, took her clothes, *and left."*

"Fuck.... Gimme a few hours. I'll head up." DeShawn's started throwing shirts and stuff into his suitcase as he talks. "I'll call Mom, see what she can do. Ok? Just... um... just hang with Jasmine for now. I'll be there later." DeShawn just hears the line go dead, no goodbye, no thanks, just silence. He finishes gathering a few more pairs of shorts and a hoodie, takes one quick look around his apartment to make sure everything is shut off and throws his bag into the pickup and starts the three hour drive. He makes it in just over two and a half hours.

"Why doesn't she love me, DeShawn? I did *everything* for her." Malik's sitting on the couch, Jasmine in his arms, bottle held firmly in his hands as Jasmine suckles on the rubber nipple.

DeShawn shrugs. "I'm sure she loves you, Malik. She's just... uh... I don't know. But I'm sure she loves you."

"She said she didn't." And Malik's eyes flit over to the small plain gold band that's still sitting on the coffee table where Deja had left it earlier that morning. "She left. Me and Jasmine. If she doesn't love me, doesn't she at least love Jasmine?"

DeShawn can see Malik's eyes getting watery and he can tell this is something that's been happening since probably before he got Malik's call earlier judging by the fact that his eyes are rimmed in red and his face is that kind of blotchy that he gets when he's worked up about something. "She loves Jasmine, and she loves you. She just doesn't know how to handle all this, I guess." DeShawn waves his hand indiscriminately around the apartment.

"Handle all this? What the fuck is that supposed to mean? All this?" Malik's voice is rising again, like it did on the phone, and Jasmine's starting to scrunch up her face, turning a very predictive shade of 'I'm about to scream my head off' red. "All this? DeShawn, I did everything for her. I cleaned this place, I cooked-well got meals ready, I did the laundry, did the errands, made all the appointments, *most of the time.*" Malik gets up, pacing with Jasmine still in his arms, bottle bouncing around and doing his best to keep the squirmy baby in his arms.

"Malik... Malik... calm down, you're scaring Jasmine." DeShawn gets up and reaches over and takes the bottle from Malik, then takes Jasmine and spends a moment cooing and comforting the baby. Jasmine seems to calm down a bit, stops stirring quite as much. DeShawn takes the empty bottle and places it on the breakfast bar before gently lifting Jasmine to his shoulder and giving her a few rubs and pats on her back. Within a moment or so, a gurgled burp comes from Jasmine and before DeShawn knows it, her little eyes are closing and her breathing is steadier against his shoulder. He takes Jasmine to the bedroom and lays her down in the crib, closing the door softly behind him as he flips on the baby monitor before returning to the living room. Malik's slumped down on the floor, back to the breakfast bar, head in his hands, leaning against his knees. His back is shaking and he's making those quiet sniffling noises again.

"I couldn't fix it, DeShawn. It didn't matter what I did. I couldn't fix it."

DeShawn slides down next to Malik and pulls his brother to him, solid arm around his back and rests his cheek against Malik's head. They may be into their twenties at this point, Malik twenty four and DeShawn twenty six, but Malik's still his little brother and DeShawn will do anything he can to make him stop hurting. Even if it's just being there for him and holding him close. DeShawn just makes non-committal noises, he doesn't know what to say anymore, what can he say? So he just tightens his arm and sits with Malik while he cries.

* * *

Malik, as much as he's loathed to leave Jasmine - he's only been away from her for about two days at the maximum at this point, is somewhat relieved as well when he has to go back to work. It's been thirty-two days since Deja left; it's hard not to count the days when your world crashes down around you and everything you thought you knew is tossed on its head, but Malik's slowly but surely finding his way back to normalcy. DeShawn had stayed with him for the first two weeks, leaving only when his mom had come down again. She'd promised to stay and help take care of Jasmine while Malik was away, and until he could find a suitable nanny. So, when he leaves on a business trip that will keep him away for at least a week, Malik's not worried one bit-well, maybe a little-but he's not *that* worried, his Mom raised three kids and Malik has implicit faith in her. Just knowing his mom is there is comfort enough.

By Christmas he's found a nanny, one who will watch Jasmine during the day when he is away at practice and will stay at his place when he'll be out late for games or away on road trips, and he's starting to feel better, more normal.

It's late January when he returns that he gets a package in

the mail-a legal sized envelope bearing the return address
of a lawyer. He can't help his hands from shaking as he
slides his finger under the envelope flap and pulls the
numerous pages of stark white paper with even starker
black printing from its enclosure; 'No-Fault Dissolution of
Marriage' petition.

Shit. He knew it was coming. He knew this was an even-
tuality. He'd heard from Deja once. *Once*. Since the day
she left in September and it wasn't her calling to say she
was sorry and that she loved him and she was coming
back. It was to tell him that she'd left for another state, had
a cousin there to live with, and that she wasn't coming
back. Malik remembers her whispering, 'I'm so sorry'
before hearing the click that comes from an actual land-
line and the deafening silence that followed. He remembers just standing there, numb. The finality of it all hitting
him like a ton of bricks.

He thanks God that they've got one home game in a few
days, then he's got a full week break before he's off for a
two-day conference. It gives him a few days to sit down,
read over the documents, and face the indisputable fact
that he is now going to be officially a twenty-four-year-old
single dad. Malik rests his forehead on the kitchen table
and just sighs.

* * *

As it turns out, the divorce petition is pretty clear cut and Malik has no objections to anything that Deja and the lawyer have outlined. Malik will receive full custody of Jasmine, no alimony is being requested, and essentially, it's just pages and pages of legalese that stating that Malik is the sole parent and provider for Jasmine going forward.

Chapter Seven

DADA

The rest of the year passes quickly.

His summer is spent back up in his childhood home, he and Jasmine riding out the warm summer months with his parents and DeShawn, his sister flitting in from time to time as she'd moved out a few summers ago and has her own life and responsibilities. Malik is now 'Dada' to Jasmine, it may be one of the only words she can say at this point, being just a month over a year old, but it melts his heart the first time she says it and he spends the better part of two days saying 'Dada' over and over to Jasmine, hoping to catch her on video saying it again. When she finally does, and she actually looks at him while saying it, rather than the toaster, the vacuum, and a rather scraggly looking squirrel that runs away in terror when Jasmine shrieks 'Dada' while pointing, Malik sends the video to literally *everyone* he knows.

And now that Jasmine is cruising around the living room, taking tentative quick little steps while holding on to the coffee table, the sofa, and Malik's big fingers for dear life, Malik finds himself putting padding, rounded corners, socket protectors, and cabinet locks on every square inch of his parents' house. DeShawn just laughs at him while his mother assures Malik that 'babies are tough, one or two bumps and bruises aren't going to break the little thing'. Malik knows he should believe her, after all, he, DeShawn, and his sister Tricia turned out just fine, but this is his little girl and he'll be damned if she so much as gets a scratch on her under his watch.

Malik's birthday comes and goes, and as August starts wrapping up, he's making tentative plans to go back to work. Jasmine is his shadow at this point, toddling around on ever steadier growing feet, pretending to talk on the phone when Malik's got his glued to his ear getting updates on clients and accounts. Jasmine's voice rises and falls with Malik's, mostly babbling and a few words here and there as Malik commiserates on the phone.

* * *

September finds Malik back home. He works hard and gets the promotion he's been after, all while still spending as much time as he can with Jasmine. Malik spends an awfully large amount of time scooping Cheerios back into the box and off the floor before chastising himself once again for leaving the box open on the table, right where Jasmine can climb up into a chair and grab it. He thinks at this point he should just buy stock in General Mills seeing as he's buying a new box every few days because he sure isn't going to let Jasmine eat floor Cheerios. DeShawn just laughs at him when he's come up to visit and tells Malik it might actually be easier to just put the freaking things away. Malik gives him the finger and calls him an asshole without thinking, then spends the next week trying to make Jasmine unlearn 'ah-hol' from her vocabulary. DeShawn just laughs even harder when Malik resorts to calling him 'a you-know-whathole'.

October comes, and Malik has no choice but to go away on an important business trip abroad, and he spends a long time kissing Jasmine goodbye and hugging her and telling him he loves her as he hands her off to his Mom-Jasmine's going to stay with Grandma and Grandpa rather than making the trip to Germany with Malik. He hates to leave her, but realizes that carting a 17-month-old baby half-way across the world to be watched over by a nanny while he works isn't exactly the most responsible thing for him to do. So, he waves goodbye to his Mom and Jasmine as they step through the security screening at the airport, before finding his own gate and heading off to Germany.

Chapter Eight

MALIK'S HOME

Malik Skypes with his parents and Jasmine at every chance he gets, his mom even taking small videos as Jasmine scribbles wildly on brightly colored construction paper with even brighter colored crayons. The pictures are nothing but tangled piles of lines, but Malik's proud of them anyway - he sets the one, his mom told him was 'Cat' as his lock screen on his phone.

Throughout his time in Germany, Jasmine's growing and changing and running and learning to feed herself with an actual spoon and Malik just sits and hopes and counts the days till he can go back home. He may be having a good time, but he'd much rather be back home, with Jasmine, seeing his baby girl at every chance he can get. Jasmine's now closing in on twenty months old and she's sitting in front of the computer, in Grandpa's lap, pointing at her nose and saying 'nose', her head and saying 'head', and at Grandpa saying 'Dada'. Malik's so proud.

Malik comes home for Jasmine's second birthday.

June rolls through, another summer spent with his parents that brings Jasmine thoroughly through her 'No' phase. Malik's pretty close to ripping his hair out-even with the family help he's got-because pretty much everything he asks Jasmine to do, ends in a resounding *no* and stomping of feet and big watery crocodile tears spilling from her huge brown eyes.

"Jasmine, it's bath time."

"No!"

"Jasmine, you have to take a bath." Malik reaches for her and she slips out of his grip, shrieking and running to hide behind DeShawn's knees. Her small fists cling to the hem of DeShawn's shorts.

"No!"

Malik takes a few steps towards Jasmine and she releases

her grip on DeShawn's shorts and turns to run, but DeShawn's quicker and scoops her up, holding her at arm's length to avoid her swinging feet as she shrieks and kicks. "Jassie... be good for Daddy and go take a bath, ok?"

Jasmine reaches for DeShawn's neck and clings to him, burying her face into his shoulder. "Don't wanna." Her voice mumbles.

"C'mon, Jassie. I'll read you a bedtime story if you go take your bath." DeShawn whispers into her ear as he brushes her curly brown hair back. "Your favorite."

Jasmine pulls her head back, tears drying on her cheeks. "Really, Uncle Dan'ie?"

"Of course, honey." DeShawn hands Jasmine over to Malik who mouths 'thanks' as he takes a very wary and still pouting Jasmine into his arms.

"We'll be quick, Jassie, then you can get all tucked in and Uncle DeShawn will read you the story-complete with the voices like you like." DeShawn rolls his eyes.

Malik hovers at the spare bedroom door-the room that used to be his growing up, but has since been turned into a make-shift Jasmine room from when she lived there while Malik was in Germany. He had bought a small bed a week or so ago, to replace the crib that would no longer hold Jasmine and her climbing, and he leans just outside the bedroom door just listening and watching as DeShawn puts on a high falsetto and reads from the well-read paperback in his hands.

*D*eShawn has plans on packing up his stuff in his old apartment, and starts looking for a place closer to Malik and Jasmine. Malik is talking to DeShawn on the phone while just relaxing out back, watching Jasmine running around in the sprinkler when he thinks he hits on a brilliant idea-one that will help both he and DeShawn out. "DeShawn, you know how you're looking for a place?"

"Yeah..."

"Well, now that you'll be with us, why don't we just get something together? This place is small and you know... it's still got... memories I guess..." Malik pauses. It's been two years since Deja walked out the door, walked out on both Malik and Jasmine, and although he's come to terms with everything, and in a way, he guesses that he realizes that this is the way it has to be, it doesn't mean that he doesn't sometimes feel some anger, regret, and sadness. He met Deja here. He found out he was going to be a father here. And his wife walked out the door here. He thinks it's time for a change-a new place and a new start. Malik hears DeShawn humming as he thinks it over.

"Yeah... yeah, that could work. I'll come up tonight so we can start looking tomorrow. I'm almost done packing here anyway."

"Cool." And they hang up.

"Jasmine, c'mere, I got some news, honey." Jasmine toddles over, brown curls wet and dripping from the sprinkler as Malik wraps her up in a big plush bath towel.

"Yeah, Daddy?" She climbs up into Malik's lap as he tousles her hair with the towel making the curls frizz and tangle.

"Your Uncle DeShawn's gonna come up tomorrow, and we're going to go look for a bigger place that we can all live together. That sound ok?" Malik's not too worried, Jasmine's still just over two years old and with all the shuffling around she's gone through-from here, with the nanny, up to Victoria and back again-he doesn't think it will take too long for her to get used to a new place-especially with her favorite Uncle living with them.

Jasmine's face lights up. "Uncle Dan'ie's coming?" She squirms down out of Malik's lap, letting the towel pool down on the concrete patio and runs in excited circles through the back yard yelling 'Uncle Dan'ie! Uncle Dan'ie!' Malik doesn't hold back his smile.

They find a place, a nice condo with three bedrooms in a pretty decent building that has a gym in the basement, a dry-cleaning service, private parking, and a residents-only pool. It's up on the fourth floor, so there's not really a backyard for Jasmine, but the place has a nice park close-by and a small-kids play area just outside the fenced in pool. Malik knows it's not going to be permanent-he'll eventually buy a house, but for now, it's something he and DeShawn can share for the next few years while they both play and Jasmine gets a bit older. Maybe once she's in school he'll look for a house, and who knows, maybe he'll have met someone by then that will be worth sharing a house with.

Not that DeShawn isn't the best company, he is, but Malik just sort of keeps it in the back of his mind that someday, when Jasmine's a bit older, he really hopes he'll meet someone that can give him a reason to love again. With Jasmine and work and life, he's been busy, and while he hasn't completely shut himself off to relationships, he's only had a handful of dates over the last year or so, but nothings lasted, and nothing even came close to love. One woman was so intent on being a mother to Jasmine that it turned Malik off so quickly they never made it past the second date. One girl was the total opposite, completely ignoring the fact that Malik had a kid and would get annoyed if Malik had to reschedule because of Jasmine. That obviously didn't last either. One or two people were pretty ok, fine with Malik having a kid, understanding that Jasmine was really his number one priority, but Malik found that after a few dates he just didn't really have any interest with them specifically, just in the feeling of having someone around that cared for him-and he realized that wasn't fair so he broke those relationships off too. This was the reason why dating Gabrielle was near unthinkable when she came into his life.

Chapter Ten

YES

They're electric. Malik and Gabrielle's friendship is strong from the start-Gabrielle moving in to the same building and it doesn't take long before she's at Malik and DeShawn's place for breakfast, lunch, and dinner and every spare moment in between that isn't spent at work. Gabrielle's great with Jasmine too-down on the carpet laying on her stomach helping Jasmine build a wobbly teetering tower of blocks, sitting with her in the overstuffed arm chair and reading any book and every book she drags off the shelves and thrusts in to Gabrielle's arms.

Gabrielle goes with them, with Malik and Jasmine, on the rare days off they have to the zoo, the park, the children's museum and she's always crouched down at Jasmine's level, pointing out how the penguins waddle back and forth then laughing when Jasmine does her best impression to match and always keeping one steady hand lightly on her shoulder when she pushes the swing back and forth as Jasmine squeals and shrieks with delight.

For the first time in years, Malik's never been happier. His career is great. His life is great. His daughter is great.

Gabrielle is great.

He stops to think about it and realizes that although it might have taken a while, his life is coming together, finally. He's got a job that he loves, a daughter that he loves-and Gabrielle. Malik realizes Gabrielle's slowly but surely working her way up to that level as well-and that's something Malik's never stopped to think about. It's just been easy with Gabrielle, she's practically a fourth member of their household, always there, always helping, always with a smile and it hits Malik-he's been slowly falling in love with Gabrielle since the minute Gabrielle walked off that plane and waved at Malik.

Finally, Malik gets the time to sit down and think about the fact that with Jasmine turning three, he really needs to make some decisions about pre-school for the fall. He also has time to think about Gabrielle.

Gabrielle had been upset when they'd lost an important client at work. But all that disappointment had faded off of Gabrielle's face when they'd trudged back through the door of Malik and DeShawn's apartment and she gathered Jasmine in her arms (after Malik had his time with her) and just hugged her and told her she missed her. Gabrielle swooping Jasmine off the floor and just holding her close with a fond smile on her face like he felt that she was something to come home to.

And the two of them, Malik and Gabrielle, also had a close relationship that had grown and grown over the last year and when Malik thinks back on all these small inconsequential memories from the last nine months; the park, the zoo, the museum, Malik realizes that Gabrielle's in every one of those memories, and when she hadn't been looking at Jasmine with that fond smile, she'd been looking at Malik the same way or had been laughing with her hand on Malik's arm or fingers around Malik's wrist pulling him off towards wherever Jasmine was running off to. *Oh.*

Chapter Eleven

FINALLY

*T*here's kids everywhere: the living room, the back yard, the hallway and the noise level hasn't gone below a dull roar for what Malik swears is well over two hours now. It's Jasmine's third birthday party, and he and DeShawn's apartment is simply overflowing with balloons, presents, snacks, deserts, and, when Malik thinks about it-love.

He makes his way in to the kitchen, looking to refill the pitcher of water that's been sitting out on the small table in the living room they'd set up for food and drinks, and to find just a split second of quiet and calm amidst the slightly controlled chaos playing out in the rest of the apartment. Malik's back is turned to the doorway, filling the pitcher so he startles a little when he hears Gabrielle's voice behind him.

"There's so many people - so many kids." Gabrielle leans against the lip of the counter next to Malik. "It's great." There's a wide smile breaking across Gabrielle's face.

"Yeah-I'm glad everyone could make it." Malik finishes filling up the pitcher, dropping another tray worth of ice cubes in to the water as he speaks.

"You doing ok with all," Gabrielle waves his hands towards the living room, the rest of the busy house, "this?"

Malik laughs a little. Malik isn't completely at ease around crowds-even if it is just family and friends. He's a quiet guy who likes quiet places and calm for the most part. "Yeah, I am. It's a good kind of crazy out there."

They're quiet for a few moments, Gabrielle drinking her lemonade, Malik just watching everything going on through the doorway-Jasmine running by at top speed squealing with DeShawn close on her heels and another group of kids trailing right behind him.

Malik turns to say something to Gabrielle but stops-Gabrielle's just looking over at Malik rather than at the goings on outside of the kitchen and her face is soft and thoughtful and happy. "Gabrielle-"

Malik's cut off as Gabrielle puts down the glass she's been drinking from and she leans in, coming in close to Malik so they're barely inches apart and Malik's eyes go wide. She hesitates for just a split second as Malik swallows and wets his lips.

The kiss soft and light and over in such a short time and Gabrielle pulls back from the kiss. "You just looked so-happy."

Malik takes a moment to reply. "I am." He looks back out to the apartment and back to Gabrielle. Malik reaches out, pulls Gabrielle back in, presses their lips together again, this time for longer, a little harder, a little more insistent, feeling Gabrielle's arms coming to rest around his waist as his own hands find Gabrielle's hips. Malik barely breaks the kiss after a few seconds, mumbling against Gabrielle's lips, "I really am."

ABOUT THE AUTHOR

Just Bae grew up in the boroughs of New York, where he was much admired for moving fast, not slow. Nowadays, he began writing in urban fiction and African American romance. Keep up with the latest news on She Got Me on FB, Instagram, and Twitter. We also would like to ask you to please leave an honest review on the platform you read this book or even multiple platforms. There are three more parts to the series and one helluva splash of an ending novel.

Many thanks!
Just Bae

91753314R00052

Made in the USA
Middletown, DE
02 October 2018